Morgan Yasbincek was born in Sydney in 1964 and settled in Perth at the age of six. She studied at Curtin University, obtained a double major in Literature and Creative Writing, and in 1993 completed Honours. In the same year she founded a committee to initiate WEB, a monthly reading and performance space for women. She is currently researching her PhD and teaching at Murdoch University.

Cover and author photograph by Stefan Szo.

To Jenny,
Thanks for having
me at Newnham '98
& for being such a
warm host.

[signature]

NIGHT REVERSING

m o r g a n   y a s b i n c e k

FREMANTLE ARTS CENTRE PRESS

First published 1996 by
FREMANTLE ARTS CENTRE PRESS
193 South Terrace (PO Box 320), South Fremantle
Western Australia 6162.

Shoreline Editors: Michael Heald and Wendy Jenkins.
Designed by John Douglass.
Production Manager Linda Martin.

Typeset by Fremantle Arts Centre Press
and printed by Quality Press, WA.

National Library of Australia
Cataloguing-in-publication data

Yasbincek, Morgan, 1964- .
      Night reversing: poetry.

      ISBN 1 86368 166 3.

      I. Title.

A821.3

Some of the poems in this book have previously been published in
a/muse, aversion, FAR, Picador New Writing 3 (Drusilla Modjeska and
Beth Yahp, eds, Pan Macmillan, 1995) and *Southern Review*.

The State of Western Australia has made an investment
in this project through the Department for the Arts.

Publication of this title was assisted by the Commonwealth
Government through the Australia Council, its arts funding
and advisory body.

contents

For the necessity of reading and being read is a dream from which we cannot awaken.

Barbara Johnson

a hundred years of sleeping

*"Enter the forest of whispery secrets said the
young and foolish girl. They touch your skin like
another responsibility."*

you can't open your eyes because the lids have
grown over
your hair carpets the room, nails coil out
heavy as horn

light sprays your retinas in grains of red
awoken lungs prompt ribs
dislocate strata of skin and dust
sensations trace over your face

you are stung by each reacquaintance
even the shape of your head has changed
the knowing is gone

senses prise at one another
angle for familiarity
a hundred years, a thousand dreams

sleeping

nose to nose, your breath
blown hot off the waters
of your blood
softens my face
dissolves into my blood

i breathe out, you breathe in
your dream translates
ciphers
                we move closer

see me

we lie awry like crash dummies
i read your eyes
close mine
see me

the fine skin at your neck jumps

my moment falls
like a drop
onto its own weight

so we sleep

tomb

i should at least have inquired about the urns
or the bandages of unravelled tongues
collected and stored

given more time it could have been painless
but you started winding early
mindful that organ removal was best
at the point of suffocation

generations of myself propped against these walls
stare at each another
death, the first blessing laid on my forehead
cracked open my epilepsy
split me like lightning

awake, accompanied, un named
my gait comically un lifelike

olfactory resonances ... a donkey
a bazaar, the smell of pink bubblegum
almost enough for a memory

most don't notice, we are perfectly preserved
our bodies divided, our death masks tranquil

white owl

as visible as the dark of the moon
you signal your presence by implication

it is only now that i sense something
of your pale wings

undetected, you had flown into me the instant
i appeared in your patterned eyes

you choose a distant perch, knowing i would come
to this suffocating dark, disoriented
driven to grief by its creatures

beg you to guide or devour me
but each step thrusts me, still unanswered
deeper into your silence

selvedge

I
hiding something

light from the refinery coats all in plasma
purple waves show blush orange teeth

foot at a time
my own enter the churning prints

sand buries itself
in its own documentation

II
orientation

to my left the road maps itself
in veins of malcontent

to my right the ocean
flounders forward

before me a print
of everything i know

but this edge plays lives on a fossil shelf
beneath which vibrancy crawls

i am my waiting
for the fringe to peel

III
ghost of a train station

crowd stands in the pattern
of these prints

scraps of torn tickets from those
who move out into the spray
gulls give the last call, so many last calls
the final rhythms round under

IV
it moves glass on glass

curled in the silence of my own
i am a colour beneath

if they stare
they have been looking for
this find

but the sea moves
on its glass

body language

here

                      no

      here

                              this wordless space

between   these words
a vibration
should touch

meet

                                  no

lower
at the fingerpoint

          of cervix

vapours smoke through organs
ignite at solar plexus condense at the imagine
trickle to hand to paper
to here

              where we are another language
              sensation and partiality
              ensures cathexis

              of memory birth
              as we pass into separation
              fiction noise

              distilled absence / watch yourself

morning

morning pauses
before letting
down
into afternoon

they can't seem to leave the sheets
— or speak
her hair reaching all over the pillow
cheek cooling against white wall
she tries to imagine a window

already concealed by voile curtains
white fence, roses on the other side
beat their own heads into the wind

her closed eyes find night blue
distant lights ignite, she straps herself in
rigid neck anticipates the ache
of a long flight

oval windows reflect interiors
where women tread the aisle
holding clutches of children's arms
like so many balloon strings

solvent images slide
over glass, against night
outside cold, him somewhere below

caught in morning
asleep across each other
they chortle like magpies

wake to cry
at the shock of yellow

death of the angel

when i found her hideout
she broke like
blown glass

fell silently
from the pages

she knew i'd come for her
come back to the diary
but not this soon

she'd prepared her testament
counter arguments

she was devoted to love
she imprisoned children

if i could pour wine for you

i think of you — a transient londoner
each day taking a puff on a cigarette
and adding one word to your construction
as perfectly as possible
as perfectly as you paint your nails

i am loathe to break
your concentration, but I could never describe
how your cat has changed since you left
smugly growing fatter
his cheeks store his wilder self
like squirrel pouches

i think of you
crouched in dark theatres
heart punching your throat
waiting to spring your wild voice
poem by poem
— and the exhaustion

if i could pour wine for you, share a moment
these thoughts would pass through me
words garnered for other things

hole in the wall

her father pushed her mother pushed her through herself

and now they wait an eternity inside the hot asbestos

for him to come home a different person

much better than he was before

now they know what's wrong with him

now his utterances are random gusts of longing that float

through the hole they love him again and he will come good

laundromat

it moves in his blood
flares across his skin

in the laundromat
he crosses his ankles
blows kisses through a cigarette
watches the round screen

forgets the woman
scaling his calf to kiss his knee
the sudden eagle
perched on rose thorns
over his shoulder

on his inner forearm a plump
naked woman standing open-palmed
is still healing

he wears her embarrassment
calmly

jack

he propped the nicotine stained beanie
on my little sister's head
said yes to a beer
no to fish and chips
and belched

mum flinched and played with her buttons
while he studied us through the ring
of his beer can

little sister didn't want to give him back
and cried when she lost the beanie
we both got a talking to

about bringing home alcoholic derelicts
which mum needed
like a hole in the head

veil

she is always somewhere
on the plain
or in the ruin

knees wide
hands on knees

like a low chair
draped in black

covered as though someone had
laid the black cloth over her
warned her

father/daughter

it was he who taught her how to shoot
now she perpetually adjusts her sights
at night she slips on her bifocals
she loves biographies

he told her one truth about her mother
who crawled through the vegetable patch
pulling grass out of hard earth

she watched the woman for forty years
and decided she'd only heard
one side of the story

he said this country has a different light
in the light of this country
memories flicker, stutter
shade reaches across to taste and take

coiled like a brain it noses across each frame
editing and feeding me in the young light
of a daughter

he said the silent censor and i play shadows
i am an instant of swallowed light and sometimes
i am jesus christ black square or the truth
a passport, thin verification of a father

this is the impossibility she almost forgets

she is teaching

my grandmother is teaching me how to bundle the wheat
we follow behind her father's scythe
she demonstrates, bent in half
her hands grabbing at the ground

she is teaching me how to store potatoes for the winter
we pile them higher than our heads
and pack them in straw and snow

my grandmother is teaching me how to polish the floor
we put rags on our feet and dance
through the minister's house

we lie still for her husband
but he still beats us and we cry over our bruises in the night

she teaches me the act of contrition, *bless me father*
for I have sinned ...

my mother is teaching me how to speak english
we stand embarrassed in a classroom
of laughing children half our size

she teaches me how to eat strawberries
— all at once in a bowl mashed in sugar
and soupy with cream

we put on our happy face, and chainsmoke
she doesn't want her name

my daughter is teaching me how
to play her game
we change the rules minute to minute

she is teaching me how to fly
we stand on a stack of slabs out the back
eyes shut, our faces to the moon

she is teaching me how to sing my work
to play *crocodile* with words
she demonstrates, hops amongst them
leaves them open behind her

other women/other messages

they began vaguely, dustings of skin cells
soap scents from one another's bathrooms

then we read his eyes for what the other
had posted
pressed a new message into his expression
with our mouths
— and he flew like mercury to deliver

we were an absurd party line
of desperate moments

i dreamt of you when you left
— you hadn't finished packing
your eyes sent their dreadful message
through me like a silver infusion

your final communication
did not slide from mouth to wire
but flew to me

the phone gave a single shriek
i knew it was you

?

it came in the late
months of the pregnancy

ian next door dug trenches
through our garden at night
hunted it from tree to earth to eaves

it cried, cried, cried
an agony, a desire

interrupted our dinner party
sent maggie home to check
her sleeping children

it threatened secrets
shoved under the serviettes
we argued over what it was

in bed at night
the folding turns
inside me
my breath, the cries

after language

our speech manoeuvres to evade it
but we are sentenced to
carry it in our syntax
never spilling a drop

except in solitude
where it undoes us from within
like a guilt of silences

becomes the fractious sounds
of those who don't make words

now almost beyond the reach of our tongues
you will be the only other to have known it
but you will never
speak of it

sole custody

her cheeks and chin wet
her hands turn the skin out and she sucks
into heart

mangoes are expensive
but are set with simpler fruits
for when she comes home

four mangoes are four white mornings
watching her fingers turn slippery

she smiles into her bites
licks orange threads
from flavescent chin
eats the ripening time

suckling deeply until
we are again waiting with a packed bag
her new elephant under her arm
the fruit basket empty

mercury

blind spin eyeless figure
your licensed confidence
contradicts metal strap-on breasts

angel of death
speak in reflection
tongue over the words that jilt you
and hold your smile

don't lie to me
she says
wading through the kitchen shadows

she cracks like a glass christmas ball
you hear bells and the summoning of gods

the last of it

we never could have expected

that our eyes would climb
like exposed spiders
seeking a crevice of familiarity

our conversation held to our chests
save a few words dropped

that when we chose a little red
we would be drinking the last of it
though it had soured black

that we would leave hungry
our car lurching and stopping
for us to fish out what was whose
from years of dim dinners

swimming amongst flotillas of
lightweight narrative that seem
too much like shots of ourselves
pretending not to notice the camera

face

first i covered my face with one hand
withdrew my head
leaving my face still fluid
with life
stretched over my palm

head to head we watched my face
wow i said afraid of the light
quivering in my hand

then you tried it
but you can never look on the face of

you got back just in time
you could have returned too late
to find the light empty and melting

night fever

the child has broken her tongue
she haunts at every periphery
opening driven cries
crashing my dream
into my chest

her tonsils flare and resist
hot, odorous
wrapped in fever

our night is awash

amphibia

I

the child in my house sings a song
about a not-too-pleased frog
unprepared for the legs
the lack
of tail
as though at seven she could imagine
what it means to be set in her ways

II

we draw at breath
as though we could smoke it
sigh over ourselves
never quite here
annoying at something left on our plate
attentions splitting, resplitting

we survive
because we are liquid, amphibious
breathing

water, air, vapour
for just another moment
but the moment is gone
and we are still kicking
to the surface

cows and bulls

i'd never have women shearers in me shed
distracts the men too much
gotta keep the cows separated from the bulls
's a man's job, women are better on the table
— more sensitive hands, got a good feel for the wool
hey, don't bloody walk away from me when I'm
talking to ya

outside the mainstreet stands in waiting for morning
a low barbed wire fence slings itself from post to post
she could probably just step over it

her nose steams, her tongue scrapes my hand for the salt
her head bones grind cud
she could probably just step over it

stepfathers

you're a package deal
handover is that intimate gesture
when they know you won't tell

their pact is made on your skin
its stain raises spies
now that you can't be trusted

they magnetise your adrenals, run them hot and cold
have to smile when they catch you out

keep you in a bottle by the bed
swallow you from the neck, vocal chords first
suck you numb
spit out love

shame

entertaining within herself she doesn't notice him

on the other side of the road until he's passed her a suspicious

look she's caught without thinking suddenly his face

is red rubber angry shouting go away go home go on piss off

there's no one else she stands drenched in his long long seconds

slides along beneath telegraph lines not looking back until

her face appears at the porthole of a green concrete bus shelter

crocodiles

she catches herself as moments;
the clap of her boot, in-breaths
droplets cross skin under her clothes

she shadows passing footfalls
                          in her own house
goes for days without speaking
                          lives on the taste of her tongue

she dreams of crocodiles
                    who wait below
like legends
for children to slip between the boards

sleeps with the lights on
spends her days poking into the dark
                          luring out the imposters
sinking, she feels her teeth
                    shut against themselves
only eyes disturb the surface

closing open

as you can see
she's slept in her clothes again
great flat arms
twist a shade about her

words are a scrutiny

she feels for her face
people say *are you ok*

all between them is inert
collapsed umbilicus

are they each cocooned
numbly sealed, hung and spinning
or packed tight winged
ready to open

she's closing open
away from the politics of sound bites
out of colour's earshot

a survival thing

her comb, bright red half-star
collapsed and blanched, face in the dirt

the yolk in the bowl
its spot of blood, tiny cornsilk thread
connects a curled white sinew
parthenogenesis?

patricia insists the rooster
two backyards away on the diagonal
jumped the fences, impregnated rosalette
and made it home undetected

the kids are off their eggs
say they smell like dead chicken

the sight of her soft as an empty pyjama bag
miniature dinosaur head propped on my forearm
blue eyelids closed

*dad says you're stupid for taking a chook to the vet
says he'd just break its neck with a shovel*

the vet says birds will conceal signs of illness
to protect themselves from the flock
usually it's too late by the time you notice
it's a survival thing

onymous

an amethyst, a worry doll
you drop the things i bring you at your feet
we empty our pockets to furnish a trail

you fray into shadow as you enter his mouth
the plane of your shoulders
the last line of you

the waiting is like
dying in a dream

when you emerge from the outsized head
his face is wormy with anger
wasps swarm his ears
you gesture to stand back

it's a secret you buzz
your arms turn papery
your head hangs like a pieta
skeletal arms slack
handless

psych rats

they can afford to be obvious
grating the floorboards to sawdust
we are at war and this signals escalation

it seems they have a leader
who lives on ratsak
and challenges the chooks
for their eggs

they are breeding as we speak
tracking through the house
on blood rinsed paws

in this exchange sanity is at stake
your skull is soft as chalk
between rodent incisors

it won't tame
its tail will grow back
it has you where it wants you

izzie's dog

I

you say you always knew
that even then you knew it was wrong
to leave the creature for dead
that you should have reported your lover
for hanging her on the letterbox

she had tried to follow
and found herself choking on his belt
snorting for breath

even then as you shut the car door
the both of you eloping, heads full of a future
her twisting body hung from the mirror
paws swimming for a surface

II

there is no hero for you
no applause for this striptease

your dog is murdered
and you have no master

you walk naked and sacred
your dirty face smiling like a saint

having experienced love as the humiliation of the soul
you must be innocent

and still your hair is not black enough
or blond enough, eyes not blue enough or brown enough

you cannot compete with the virgin in the pink angora cardigan
or the best fuck he ever had

III

you re-read her
and commit rituals over her books
trying to bring her into your skin

if only you believe hard enough

your eyes develop an irritation
the red makes the green iridescent

you want to die like her
anorexic and pure

you eat raw soaked chickpeas and poached egg whites
you drink air through yellow teeth

you would give anything to see your dog again

IV

when she comes back
she runs all the way
her lungs raw and heaving
she runs to her second chance
like an escapee laughing

her spaniel screams
leaps waist-high on seeing her again

she takes her dog
nothing but the clothes on her back
and her dog

stories

set adrift ice ages ago
we live on the bones of other's stories
look out from the coasts
try to get closer to screens

the wind blows backward
summer hair in cold face
seasons twitch

stories of a homeland
backwash off the ears of grandparents
great grandparents

stories magical enough
for them to have put aside for years
for the fare

The People search cities on the fringe of a heartland
for their stolen children

others speak mother tongues in small groups
alien intonations turn ears away

these stories blow about under feet
like fine top soil

rottnest resort

here we are offered vantages on our faery city
resplendent, glowing like burning ash, from across the ocean
we are lords of our time, own every minute here
having negotiated an attractive history

amongst the salt sewer smell of rotting seaweed
in the teeth of a graveyard
we stick close to the buildings, prefer the sun's hard slap

to the twisted shock of black tree shadow
where marsupials tamed by disease
bite their mange
cyclists swoop over roads
pink lakes spit froth and turn inward
birds make their noises at night

your neck cleaved almost to the bone
you take a hundred years to walk to my window
knock
send me back to the mainland
your wounds hot sting behind glass

january

can't sleep
heat crickets ring
unanswered

thoughts thrash
in the humidity
having fallen from the sky:
write, work, parent, drive, repair the house
fifteen minutes to find this journal
this room lost in personal things
impaled futures
pressure

woken is the place
where all is assembled;
antidotes to fear locate
death and disease
outside the privileged are overwhelmed
if only by the struggle of their seclusion

night reversing a dawn reversing
sprinklers tap dry air with scent
the little mandarin tree sprays back citrus
mosquitoes emerge from grainy light
float like sylphs
and the fish are *still* falling

Canada Poems

You are about to enter your own script, you are about to become
your verisimilitude, you are about to cross the international date
line. You are flying at 36000 feet. You are asked to observe the
no smoking sign, you have a choice of beverages with lunch,
you must fasten your seatbelt. You have a lifejacket under your
seat. In case of emergency the oxygen mask will drop automati-
cally; you are asked to calmly make your way to the exit in an
orderly fashion. You have a choice of nine music channels;
select your channel from the panel on your seat, enjoy your
flight. The plane is an armour beyond trojan dreams, a rescuer
with refugees in its belly; the dragon screams, lifts you up out of
a life, out of a city, out of a country; so many stories continue in
the absence of their characters. You drag your neck forward, sit
up, look at the other passengers.

Four hours to the other side of the country, just like when we
were kids: now it's night, o.k. now everybody go to sleep. o.k.
now it's morning, wake up everybody, let's gather breakfast
from the jungle ... Hey! You just walked through the wall ...
i am woken from a dream, a disturbing, bitter dream of discord,
argument to enter another which contains it, like an atmos-
phere. Am I leaving a city, a country, or a dream? The plane
rolls on its side, Sydney.

An American couple in the next aisle keep standing to check
their matching Akubra hats in the overhead locker, at the sound
of the latch their heads enter the aisle. They are the same
person. The woman half is more active, speaks to the stewards,
the passenger, opens little plastic food packets on the trays,

adds sugar to their coffees, stirs. The man half watches her, his tray pokes his belly, his arm levers up and down, she orders them second meals. A Japanese man walks a crying child up and down the dim cabin, anxious, pursued by an invisible pack of vicious screaming-kid-on-the-plane stories. Child sleeps across my lap, floats slightly above her body, beyond the freezing black at the window, flits close to the sun, cheeks burn deep pink from the sun, hair on forehead, neck slick, dark, moist, mouth opens, pouts, gently suckles a giant invisible breast.

Already things are strange. A single cloud has stayed in my window from somewhere in the Pacific to Vancouver. I slept with my back to it, but it entered through a dream and took me to a place ... a place I know ... but cannot remember ... It must be a dream ... or an angel.

Her mother explains to another passenger that they are four generations, from great grandmother to great granddaughter. The passenger seems pleased, but notices that the issue is con-tentious; for there are silences held down between the women, suffocating the spaces between them.

*   *   *

4 a.m.? My baby won't sleep, her sense of time has been turned inside out. Her insomnia haunts me. It spears my dreams and they thrash around me as I open my eyes. Her eyes are dark openings, their moist edges catch the light. My body is angry for sleep. We are not welcome here. Somehow we have

intruded. There have been scenes with strangers. Both sides, two families open themselves to each other in gesture, yet they are complete strangers. They say — we have heard so much, we feel as if we know you. We are completely preceded. Our mouths are stitched, but they want to photograph our bodies, they want our bodies to appear at important events, at the wedding. We are trapped in a drama, there's no off button, remote control is not for the remote, and the sponsors pay generously. She is too young to whisper quietly. I take her upstairs. We sit on the lounge. There is not enough light to make colour in the room.

In Canada you will hear 'bathroom', but not that word, the one we use as a matter of fact, as functional mundane reality. No matter how much of an aside you thought it was, it will flush away the rest of your story, stirring up embarrassed glances, and, yes surprised as you may be, you did press the button.

We walk through the ravine; a path stoops down to follow the banks of a small stream. The path is moist and spongy with red and orange matter, a child's drawing of a pizza. The trees settle in to pose for winter, plead against their naked thinness. You could forget the spring secret of their deepest veins. She wants to photograph me. I get her to stand in the leaves, set the camera. She's impatient, she keeps breaking out of camera window, toward me, wants the camera. I show her through lens, make it blur, clear, blur. See, I need to make the picture clear. She goes back to her position. I kneel, try to approximate her height while I focus. I take the camera from my face, she steps forward, wait until I get to where you are. I give her the camera. She doesn't want instructions. She goes to where I was focusing. I am kneeling in the leaves. She stands legs apart, elbows out, camera almost completely hides her face. She doubts nothing about what she's doing. I laugh, she takes the photo.

We look out for skunks, people here dread their spray. The daily bath in tomato juice for a couple of weeks will only cut the edge from the smell. The oil enters the skin itself, remains noticeable for as long as six months. My sister says she can smell skunk, I cannot identify a pervasive scent.

We walk the bend in the ravine. Autumn is a bold challenge to spring; trembling, loud, yellow. The whole of this country is in love with the sky. They are shouting at one another here, avoiding one another there, and ecstatic to each other's touch here. We are from a land where thoughts are sunk deep before they touch its waters, yet in places, she surfaces, thrusts open, floats, and sinks again. Her body is the vibration of the didgeridoo, calling, calling in concentric circles. Her coils are tight in sacred spaces, enter and she waits over you, like a mother giving warning. You know she can strike you, your body beats, you never speak aloud or sing here.

A grey building sits above, like a concrete castle on a boulder. It is being demolished, yet it seems indestructible. It is as solid as a hive of bomb shelters and it reeks of atrocity. It had been the only slaughterhouse for swine in the province, millions of pigs were butchered here. Their blood still gives it life. I can see canals of it flowing through the slaughterhouse, regulating a rhythm of fear and death. Pigs enter, are stunned by the smell, the death, their death magnified by millions of others. It consumes the building, takes the concrete monster for a body, a giant legless form, weak with its own gorging; taking in screaming pigs, passing out blood, entrails, ground bone and packed meat.

I remember a man entering a holding pen for six or so pigs. He took one between his legs, punched its throat. A long thin knife blade came away with his hand, followed by a thick river of blood, pig groaning, pig lying on its side, hind quarters cycling, trying to get up, pig staring at its blood in the dirt, pig tiring, a wind-up toy left on its side, pigs barging the corner of the pen, squealing, panic, panic, panic, pig dragged from the pen, hot bath, shaved, pig soft, pig mute, pig death.

What it means to be called a pig, what it means to be treated like a pig, they thought they knew pig.

No one mentions the tree opposite, opening its living yellow with the light.

A wedding 'shower'.
Seated at the long table in this order: bridesmaid, bridesmaid's daughter, bride, mother of the bride, mother-in-law. Sixty chairs semi-circle the table. On each chair sits a woman. The women introduce themselves in turn. Just outside the semi-circle another trestle table is layered with gifts. The gifts are carried from the gift table to the head table by the bride's future sisters-in-law. The bride opens the card, thanks the woman responsible for the gift, passes the card to the head bridesmaid who notes the name of the gift giver. The head bridesmaid then watches as the bride opens the gift and notes the gift next to the name. The gift is held up for the women sitting in the semi-circle to see. The gift is passed around the semi-circle, examined by each woman, and taken back to the gift table. Ribbons are taken from the gifts and tied onto a paper plate to make a bonnet which the bride puts on when all the gifts have been presented. Then the women are invited to eat and drink food provided by

the women of the groom's family. The bride will respond in writing to their gifts within a couple of weeks, thanking each personally.

Today my grandmother is restless. She has brought forth a creature from her journey into sleep. It is dark and it squats between her shoulder-blades. She is silent. When she looks to whoever is speaking to her, her eyes turn to her back, as though she is ashamed of it. Finally it speaks, or dances. Her dream from the night before unfolds from her back, drops to the floor in a long thin ribbon, then curls upward into a spiral staircase, a black cross sits at its peak. The dream is surprisingly rude to the old woman. It orders her to climb the stairs alone. She stands singled out among the many spectators who have gathered, knowing she can't make it. She begins the climb ... soon she is crying with the pain of it. No one else can access the stairs now. She cannot come down. I sit with her on the sofa, angry at the smug dream resettling on her back. I hold her, her eyes glance over mine, wishing she could trust my comfort.

Canada man who leans hard on his accent, moose hunts on the weekend, and who sneers at 'bellyaching greenies', will warn you about the bears,

and the woman bak'n pie for the trip opens their dishwasher with her thumbs so as not to split her acrylic nails.

The Canada man likens himself to the grizzly. Initiated by older men. His first hunt at puberty, young as fourteen or fifteen ...

intoxicated by blood,
by uncles' stories,
by graphic moments
of open skin,

hands sort through
warm organs,
the blade
slipped beneath
the skin,
blood taste
of raw liver,
they come,
a trophy from the gore.

Those Canada grizzlies on the dancefloor really say, you're just
about the sweetest thing I ever did see. Identifiable bear
uniform: blue jeans, baggy crotch, baseball caps, unless they
really do have hair. They heave themselves round and round,
swinging on their partners. Lone Star Saloon cave bears dance
on, no photos allowed. Well shit, who's going to believe there
really are bears here if I can't take a photo? It's true what they
say about grizzlies, they're loners, and they love the smell of
blood. You just do not camp amongst them if you're bleeding.
You can tell the ones after blood. They want you to look at their
wounds first.

The cloud visited today, in the shower, the space occupied,
invisibly. A harmony touched breasts with its breath, folded
itself down my belly, snaked further. Both soapy hands opened
onto the glass, head heavy and dark, streaming water, a dark
weedy moon on the glass. The bathmat, mirror, floor were left
wet, tropical.

A feathered headdress announces the first warnings from a
glass case at the entrance. Broad white feathers fall away from a
beaded headband; feathers from creatures who fly for creatures

to fly, to make wings, to perch on a brow. Feathers gathered
before my mother was born, feathers gathered for ritual.

My daughter refuses to enter the exhibit. A single feather could
shatter the security glass.

A single feather which tipped the winds thousands of metres
above the museum, which shook behind the heels of the one
who wore it, hangs from the head of a mannequin in a glass
case.

Mannequins with black plaited hair, faces and hands painted
gloss red-brown, wear someone else's buckskin hide clothes.
Their faces take the physical space of someone else's faceless-
ness. The eyes are as expressive as the hands, the painted on
teeth, they are dolls less magical than their dress.

Pouches of skin lie unfolded on the other side of the glass.
Rattles, pipes, feathered wands bound with thonging, beads,
stones, rest on the skin. Next to these ritual tools, the
headdress, clothes, moccasins of the one, the only one autho-
rised to use them. The tools form a bundle. Each bundle
represents a specific ritual which only the owner of the bundle
may perform. For each tool in the bundle there is a correspond-
ing spirit represented and called upon.

The owner of the bundle mediates between the spirits and the
tribe in the actualising of ritual. The spirits don't recognise us.
We are a confusion of respect, knowing now we should never
have laid eyes on the bodies of the spirits — exposed behind
glass. Their singing was entirely inaudible, entirely effective.
Only the child had known what to do.

A large, pale circle has appeared in the center of my palm. I once heard that this is an indication of blindness. In the hope of finding a point of reference I write a letter to myself and address it to my friend. My senses are jammed. I cannot get back.

Whenever we go anywhere we have to discuss the possibilities of the directions we've been given; what they seem to mean, what they could possibly mean. We are finding our way into unfamiliar streams, in our attempt to decode the spatial logic, we are always lost, until we find a destination.

There must be another space, another gathering, another country where we should have met, where you could consolidate form and could speak, where you could recognise yourself, where you could alight my hopes, leave them hanging like bats for me to collect after sleep. If i were a night sky, there would be nothing to say, my stars would make you dream, my moons would draw you away from the earth, and still we could not touch. There would only be a dialogue of vibration, only a straining, a reaching into the widening space. If i were earth and grass, there would be mountains where we touched and mist where you lie against my skin. Where is this place? Where is this place?